GREAT BIG
SOFTIE

Kaye Baillie

Shane McG

NEW FRONTIER PUBLISHING

Elliot **looked**
like a monster.

He **sounded**
like a monster.

He even **smelled**
like a monster.

GREAT BIG
SOFTIE

For Jacob, Charlie, Harry and Fletcher ~ K B

For Buddy ~ S McG

First published in Great Britain in 2022
by New Frontier Publishing Europe Ltd
Uncommon, 126 New King's Rd, London SW6 4LZ
www.newfrontierpublishing.co.uk

A CIP catalogue record for this book is available from the British Library.

ISBN: 978-1-913639-72-3

Edited by Tasha Evans
Designed by Verity Clark

Printed in China
1 3 5 7 9 10 8 6 4 2

But deep down inside his
big monster belly...

Elliot was a
GREAT BIG SOFTIE.

All the other monsters were **TROUBLE**.

They **dribbled.**

They **trampled.**

They **burped.**

BURP!
BURP!

Elliot did not like doing
any of those things.

But how else would
he ever fit in?

Elliot decided it was time to

monster up.

He took a deep monster breath, then...

'Don't call me sweetie!'

'RAAARRRR!'

'Oh, dear!' cried the shopkeeper. 'What a mess.'

Next, Elliot stomped up to a churros van.
'I'll be right with you, pal.'